D1432526

STARDUST
SCHOOL OF
D☆NCE

PRIYA the Swan Queen

FIVE MILE

Five Mile
the publishing division of Regency Media
www.fivemile.com.au

First published 2020

NATIONAL
LIBRARY
OF AUSTRALIA

A catalogue record for this
book is available from the
National Library of Australia

ISBN: 9781925970685 (paperback)
Printed in Australia by Ovato 5 4 3 2 1

STARDUST
SCHOOL OF
D☆NCE

PRIYA the Swan Queen

BY ZANNI LOUISE
ART BY SR. SÁNCHEZ

FIVE
MILE

CHAPTER ONE

Priya was busy drawing on a piece of paper. It was Monday. Sun streamed into the classroom window, draping her paper in gold.

Priya was meant to be reading silently about Vikings. Instead, she was drawing a dog in a tutu. The dog looked like Priya's own dog, Petit Jeté. Except its ears were bigger and its nose was longer.

Priya giggled at her drawing. It came out like a piglet snort.

Priya's new teacher, Mrs Huff, looked up sharply from her desk. Mrs Huff's lips made a walnut shape.

She shook her head at Priya.

'Do you find Vikings very funny, Priya?' asked Mrs Huff.

'Not really,' said Priya softly. She hated getting into trouble.

Priya rubbed out her dancing dog. She focussed on the page about Vikings. She tried to at least.

For Priya, the words were just a bunch of sounds.

She knew some of the words. But most words Priya had to sound out, letter by letter, in her head.

By the time she got to the bottom of the page, she had forgotten most of what she had read.

Priya's heart beat faster. *What if Mrs Huff asks me about Vikings?* she thought. *Even worse, what if Mrs Huff asks me to read aloud?*

Priya tried remembering everything she already knew about Vikings. *Er, nothing.*

She flicked through the textbook, looking for pictures and diagrams. They might give her some clues.

But there were no pictures or diagrams. The book was just words, words, words.

Urgh! I'm never going to know anything about Vikings.

A voice broke into Priya's worried thoughts. It was Mrs Huff.

'Priya Patel, I said can you please come up the front and read your favourite paragraph aloud?'

Mrs Huff was standing over Priya's desk, with her hands on her hips.

'Aloud?' whispered Priya. 'In front of the whole class? But ... I can't.' Her voice disappeared.

'Can't is not a helpful word,' said Mrs Huff. 'Up you get, Priya, please.'

'But ... I need to go to the bathroom,' said Priya.

'Priya, you went to the bathroom ten minutes ago. Now, come read for us.'

Priya shuffled to the front of the classroom. She closed her eyes. She tried to imagine she was at Stardust School of Dance instead of standing in front of her whole class about to read.

Shoulders back, her dance teacher, Madam Martine, would always say.

Imagine a string pulling your head to the sky. Now breathe.

Priya breathed in, then out. She slumped as she began to read. 'The ... V-v-i-k-ings ... where—'

Someone sniggered.

Priya looked up.

Dennis Hobbs was covering his mouth.

'The Vikings,' Priya started again, 'where ...' She stopped. Her head pounded. Her eyes stung. Priya wished she could zap home right now, curl up with Petit Jeté and sleep for a hundred years.

'I'll read, Mrs Huff!' someone called out from the front row. It was Mandy Wellwish, one of the smartest kids in Priya's class. Mandy was waving her hand around like a helicopter propeller.

Mandy to the rescue, thought Priya.

Before Mrs Huff had a chance to say anything Priya rushed back to her seat.

'Very well, Mandy. Come and read,' Mrs Huff said with a sigh. 'Priya, make sure you do your nightly reading practice. It will make all this much easier.'

Priya blinked back tears. *It won't*, she thought. *It never gets easier*.

'The Vikings *were* ...' Mandy Wellwish started reading and Priya's thoughts drifted back to Petit Jeté wearing a tutu. It was a much happier thought than having to read in front of the class.

That afternoon Priya was leaning against the school gate, waiting for her mum.

She saw Mrs Huff. The teacher was monitoring the bus queue, and waving kids goodbye.

Soon, Priya heard some quick footsteps. She recognised them right away. Priya's mum always took speedy steps. She was a busy vet, at a busy vet clinic, so school pick-ups always had to be done quick smart.

Priya and her mum were walking off down the street when Mrs Huff called after them.

'Mrs Patel, may I please have a word?' called Mrs Huff.

Uh-oh, thought Priya.

'I'm sorry. I have to get back to the clinic, Mrs Huff. Can it wait until tomorrow?' asked Priya's mum.

'Just quickly,' said Mrs Huff, 'I think it's really important you put aside an extra thirty minutes each evening to help Priya build her reading confidence. We don't want her falling behind.'

Priya tried to send her mum a secret message without words. *No more reading. Please, Mum!*

'Absolutely,' said Mrs Patel, taking Priya's hand and giving it a squeeze. 'I completely agree. We will put in 150 percent. Won't we Priya?'

Priya sighed, but didn't say anything.

Doesn't Mum know I'm already putting in 150 percent?

Maybe even 200 percent. It just doesn't matter how hard I try, Priya thought glumly, *I am not a good reader.*

'All right, goodbye, Mrs Huff,' said Priya's mum.

Priya waved to her teacher.

'Come, Priya,' said her mum, grabbing Priya's hand as they hurried together down the street. 'I have a surprise for you at the clinic.'

CHAPTER TWO

The surprise Priya's mum had waiting for Priya was truly wonderful.

It was an alpaca called Mavis! She was munching grass in the little yard behind the vet clinic.

'Oh, I love her!' said Priya, wrapping her arms around Mavis's woolly neck. 'But, Mum, why is she here?'

'A lovely man called Bob brought her in,' said Priya's mum. 'He found her on the side of the road. Bob can't look after her though, so we have to think of a solution.'

'I'll look after her!' said Priya at once. 'She can live in our backyard! I'll feed her every day. And brush her. And talk to her. And keep her warm—'

'Slow down, Priya,' said her mum, laughing. 'Our backyard is tiny. And you already have a million animals.'

'Only six, Mum!' said Priya, holding up her fingers to count:

'Petit Jeté, Crayon, Quacky, Marshmallow, Tiger and Snow. There's room for Mavis! She can keep the guinea pigs company!'

'I don't know,' said her mum.

'Just until she finds another home?' begged Priya. 'Oh, pretty please, Mum! I'll do anything!'

Priya's mum was quiet and looked deep in thought. Priya made her best pleading puppy-dog eyes.

'Fine,' said Priya's mum, at last. 'Just until we find Mavis another home. And on one condition. You need to promise me you will do that extra half-hour of reading.

Every night. Okay, Priya? You can't let Mavis be a distraction. And I am also going to book you in with that reading tutor Edmund's mum suggested. Zac Maxwell.'

By now Priya was only half listening. She had heard the important bit. Mavis the alpaca was moving in!

Priya tickled Mavis's chin. Mavis nibbled her hand. Priya giggled.

'It's a deal,' said Priya. Anything to take Mavis home. Even reading. That's how adorable Mavis was!

Later that afternoon, Priya was in the backyard trying to tie an old blanket around Mavis's middle. She didn't want Mavis to get a cold tummy while she slept.

Priya's sausage dog, Petit Jeté, was jumping up and down. He was trying to lick the alpaca's body. But Mavis kept shuffling away. From Petit Jeté. And from the old blanket.

'Hold still, Mavis,' said Priya gently. 'Try to imagine there is a string, pulling your head to the sky.'

Priya demonstrated for Mavis. While she was in her ballet stance, Priya pointed her toe forward.

Mavis watched through her long eyelashes as Priya did spring points. Then, the cutest thing ever – Mavis stuck her hoof forward!

'You can do spring points, Mavis!' said Priya, laughing. 'Wait until I tell the others at dance class tomorrow!'

'Guess what, Priya?' said Priya's younger sister Shaan, appearing at the back door.

Shaan had just got back from gymnastics and was still in her leotard. She did a perfect cartwheel across the backyard.

'I don't know. You got another gold sticker in class today,' said Priya.

'Nope,' said Shaan. 'Even better. I got a certificate for "Most Conscientious Student." Do you know what "conscientious" means, Priya?'

'Um,' said Priya, focussing on

tying the blanket, 'biggest bragger?'

Shaan was always getting certificates. Priya had never got any. It wasn't fair.

'Muuum!' wailed Shaan. 'Priya called me a bragger.'

Their mum came into the backyard. Her mobile phone was pressed to her cheek. She flapped her hand at Priya and Shaan to be quiet.

'Yes. Uh-huh,' Priya's mum said into the phone. 'Great. Tuesday. 4.30. Wonderful. Can you text me the address? Thanks so much, Zac. Bye!'

'Good news, Priya,' said her mum, slipping the phone in her pocket. 'Zac Maxwell can squeeze you in on Tuesdays.'

'But, but ... Tuesdays are Stardust days!' said Priya.

Mavis's blanket dropped to the grass. Mavis trotted away from it, to where the guinea pigs live.

'Well, Priya, it's the only day Zac can do,' said her mum. 'He's super busy. And we are lucky to get an appointment at all. Reading is important, darling.'

'So is dance,' grumbled Priya.

She whipped up the blanket and

folded it roughly in a bunch. Priya wasn't going to make Mavis wear a blanket if she didn't want to. If only her parents wouldn't make her read.

'Well, Zac isn't available until next Tuesday,' said her mum, gently. 'So you have one more week of dance class. That will give you a chance to let your dance friends know. You can always arrange catch-ups outside of class.'

Priya ran off to her bedroom feeling sorry for herself. Petit Jeté followed, close at her heels.

CHAPTER THREE

The next afternoon, Priya was sitting in the back seat of her mum's car, with Petit Jeté huddled on her lap. They were driving down Blossom Lane on the way to Stardust School of Dance.

'Please, Mum,' pleaded Priya from the back seat, 'maybe you can find another tutor.'

'We've been through all this,

Priya,' said her mum. 'Dance will still be there. Let's get your reading up. Then you can come back to Stardust later in the year.'

Usually Priya skipped into dance class. But today she was like a sick, ancient tortoise. She slumped up towards the little wooden dance hall. Her mum walked alongside her.

Petit Jeté ran ahead. He knew where he was going. He ran straight through the open yellow door. From the street, Priya could hear his little paws tip-tapping across the wooden floorboards.

Madam Martine appeared at the doorway and she practically threw herself at Priya.

'Priya! Finally, you are here!' said Madam Martine. She sounded very excited. 'Come! I have such magnificent news!'

'Madam Martine,' said Priya's mum briskly. 'I need to talk to you about something. Priya—'

But Madam Martine cut her off. 'Mrs Patel, with all due respect, the students are already warming up. I prefer to speak with parents after class, so I can give you my undivided attention. Until then!'

Madam Martine took Priya's hand, and pulled her into the hall.

Inside, Priya's best friend, Bertie, was leading the other dancers. Edmund and Lulu followed behind Bertie as she moved around the room.

Priya and Petit Jeté ran to join them. Bertie skipped. The others copied. Bertie twirled. So did the others. Even Petit Jeté did his best to join in.

Priya smiled as she twirled. The yucky feeling washed away. She wasn't a sick tortoise anymore.

She was a butterfly! A dragon! A swan! She could almost feel wings growing on her back. She could feel them stretch wide.

When Priya danced she thought only about dancing.

She couldn't think about bad things. She couldn't think about reading, or Mrs Huff, or Dennis Hobbs.

She couldn't even think about this being her last dance class for a while.

'Marvellous dancers, please form a circle on the floor,' said Madam Martine, clapping to get their attention. 'I will tell you my exciting news while you stretch!'

Priya sat beside Bertie, and Petit Jeté squiggled onto Priya's lap.

'The Animal Rescue Society has asked us to perform at their fundraiser in the park in two weeks' time,' said Madam Martine. She gazed directly at Priya as she spoke.

'Wow! We can dance to help animals!' shouted Priya, excitedly. But her grin faded. She remembered that she couldn't be there for the Animal Rescue dance. She wouldn't even be there for the next dance class.

Priya's wings curled up tight, and *ZAP!* disappeared.

'That's right, Priya,' said Madam Martine, smiling her widest smile.

'The fundraiser will help many animals. Of course, it must be a dance we can do outdoors. Any thoughts?'

'Priya should choose the dance!' said Lulu. 'She is obsessed with animals.'

Priya bit her lip.

'*Peter and the Wolf* has lots of animals in it!' said Bertie, nudging Priya with her elbow.

'But we've already done that one,' said Edmund. 'Why don't we do something new, Priya?'

Priya looked at the floor.

'Can everyone please stretch

their feet towards the centre and try to reach their toes?' said Madam Martine.

Priya stretched and shut her eyes tight.

'*Swan Lake* is about animals,' Priya heard Madam Martine say.

'But *Swan Lake* is too sad!' said Lulu with a loud sniff.

Priya looked up from her stretch to see Lulu's eyes welling up. Knowing Lulu, she was replaying the whole ballet in her imagination.

Swan Lake was Priya's favourite ballet.

Yes, it is a sad ballet, Priya thought. *But the saddest thing is that whichever dance Stardust perform, I won't be part of it.*

'I have something to tell you all,' said Priya. Her voice croaked a little.

CHAPTER FOUR

Bertie, Lulu and Edmund squeezed Priya so tight, she thought she was going to pop.

Petit Jeté nosed his way into the group hug too.

Priya's friends were all very sad that she wasn't going to be at Stardust for a while.

Even Madam Martine gave her a big cuddle.

'I have a feeling that you will be back at Stardust sooner than you think, Priya,' Madam Martine whispered.

When Priya got home, she and Petit Jeté headed out to the backyard. Priya brought her dad's tablet with her.

Petit Jeté started running in circles. Quacky the duck waddled after him. Crayon the cockatiel watched from her perch. The three guinea pigs – Tiger, Marshmallow and Snow – nibbled grass in their cage. Mavis the alpaca munched on Priya's dad's strawberries.

Priya watched the animals for a few moments before sitting under the mulberry tree.

She typed 'AMINL RESKU SOSITY' into her dad's tablet. She wanted to find out more.

'Your search AMINL RESKU SOSITY did not match any doc-doc-u-ments,' Priya read slowly.

I must be spelling it wrong, she thought.

She tried again. AMINLE RESQU SOSITY

Still no results. This time Priya sounded each letter out as she typed. ANIML RESCU SOSIETY

Finally, the words: 'Did you mean ANIMAL RESCUE SOCIETY?' popped up on her screen. So did hundreds of search results.

'This must be it!' said Priya, clicking open the first website link.

It was the Animal Rescue Society website. As well as pictures, there were lots of words.

Priya scrolled past the paragraphs and clicked on an image of headphones.

It was handy this website could read aloud to her.

In her backyard that afternoon, Priya heard some really sad stories about animals.

She wiped her tears away with the back of her hand.

'Petit Jeté, come here immediately!' said Priya. She wrapped her dog in a cuddle. 'Can you believe there are animals without people to love them?'

Mavis also trundled over, and licked the top of Priya's head.

'Thank goodness Bob found you when he did, Mavis!' said Priya, looking up at the alpaca.

After hearing the sad stories, Priya realised that the Animal Rescue fundraiser was even more important than she had first thought. She knew now she had to help raise money for the animals to help them find safe and happy homes. She just had to!

Priya remembered that Madam Martine had said the performance would be the following Sunday.

Maybe, if I do all my reading homework, and try 150 percent at Zac Maxwell's lessons too, Mum will let me join in next Sunday. I could rehearse at home. I could meet my friends out of class to practise. A plan was taking shape in Priya's head.

'I can do it, Mavis!' said Priya, hugging the alpaca's neck. 'I can help fundraise for the Animal Rescue Society! I know I can.'

She gave Petit Jeté and Quacky a cuddle too. She didn't want them to feel left out.

'There you are, Priya!' called Priya's dad from the back door. 'I picked up some great books from the library during my lunch break. Come inside and let's read some exciting stuff!'

Priya rolled her eyes at her animals. 'I guess fun time is over,' she told them. 'Let the hard work begin!'

Priya followed her dad inside, past Shaan who was reading a giant book at the dining table.

It probably has tiny little letters and billions of words, thought Priya.

'I've read those books a million times,' said Shaan, glancing at the pile of books on the coffee table.

'Hush, Shaan,' said her dad. 'Priya doesn't need to hear that. It will kill her confidence.'

Confidence? thought Priya. She didn't have any confidence when it came to reading. Priya felt like a toddler when she read aloud. A very unconfident toddler.

'This book looks fun!' said Priya's dad, plonking onto his big chair. 'Read me a story, Priya!'

Priya sighed and sat down. She knew her dad was trying to make reading fun. Reading was such a big effort for Priya, but she didn't want to disappoint her dad.

Pressing her finger under each word, she sounded out the title

of the book. 'How to build rocket skips,' she read slowly.

'Ships,' corrected her dad. 'Rocket ships.'

'Rocket ships,' repeated Priya.

Petit Jeté lay down across Priya's feet. It was his way of telling her that he understood, and that he would make life as nice for her as he could.

Priya smiled at Petit Jeté, and turned back to the book.

Thirty minutes of reading creaked by like a rusty wheel. Priya sounded out words as best she could. Often, the sounds got stuck in her throat.

Like they were trapped. But Priya kept thinking: *150 percent, Priya. Then maybe you can help the animals at the fundraiser.*

'Sorry, Dad,' muttered Priya as she stumbled over 'spanner' for the fourth time. 'I'm tired.'

Her dad patted her knee and smiled.

'You did really well, Priya. And tomorrow will be even easier!'

'I don't think so, Dad. But I'll do my best,' said Priya.

When at last reading time was over, Priya went to her room. She pulled out a fresh piece of paper and her drawing pencils.

The blank paper gave Priya a magical empty feeling. It felt like it was washing away all the words crammed inside her.

Priya started to hum.

She knew the music from *Swan Lake* well because Madam Martine often played it during classical ballet lessons.

As Priya hummed, her pencil danced across the page. Pictures of a girl with swan wings seemed to fall out of her pencil.

Priya hummed louder and her pencil moved quickly.

She drew the swan girl pirouetting, then leaping across the page. Her wings spread out, as she flew to a new page. Page after page, the swan girl danced.

Priya didn't need words to tell her version of *Swan Lake*.

It was the story of a girl who couldn't write or speak, but she could dance beautifully with her swan wings ... and that is what made her the Swan Queen!

CHAPTER FIVE

Priya was eating porridge with her family on Friday morning.

'Mum,' said Priya. 'You know how I have been reading every night with Dad?'

'Yes,' said Mum. 'So proud of you, darling!'

'Well, do you think I could join the Animal Rescue fundraiser dance in the park?' asked Priya.

'It's just … I have a good idea for the dance,' Priya quickly added. 'I can teach the others outside of class. We can all practise on our own.'

'Maybe Madam Martine could organise an extra class so you can go along,' said her mum, thinking aloud. She grinned at Priya. 'Dancing to save animals, hey? I can't see how you could miss that!'

It turned out that Madam Martine was happy to organise a special class for Priya to share her idea for the fundraiser.

In fact, Madam Martine was able to organise for Priya to meet Bertie, Edmund and Lulu at the Stardust dance hall that very afternoon.

'Your mum said you have a dance for us for the fundraiser, Priya,' said Madam Martine. 'She said you'd re-written *Swan Lake*. To make it happier for Lulu.'

'Actually, I have re-*drawn Swan Lake*,' said Priya, pulling a wad of paper out of her bag.

She lay the dance sequences, scene by scene, across the floor. Bertie held Petit Jeté, so he wouldn't walk all over Priya's hard work.

'This,' said Priya, pointing to the first page, 'is Odette, the prima ballerina in *Swan Lake*. Here she is just a girl who can't talk. And she can't read and write. She's moving sadly beside the lake.

'And this,' continued Priya, pointing to the second page, 'is when Odette finds a cygnet, which is a young swan, alone by the water. Odette can't call to the cygnet

because she doesn't have words.
So she picks it up and dances with
it. The swan thinks Odette is its
mother.

'This one,' said Priya, 'is where
the swan gives Odette her magic to
say thank you. Odette is dancing
home when she realises that wings
are growing from her back.

'At first Odette is scared, but then she realises that she can fly! That makes her the Swan Queen.

'In this scene, Odette flies around the lake, enjoying her new wings.'

'She could do a glissade!' sang Lulu, who knew lots of French words for ballet steps. 'Or a chassé. They are both very graceful.'

'She could leap through the air,' said Bertie, 'or do an aerial flip!'

Priya pointed to the last page. 'Odette sees a baby bird, stuck in a tree and flies up to help it. The bird and Odette dance around the lake. The cygnet joins in.

'As they are dancing,' Priya said, 'they see a little squirrel stuck in a trap. Odette and the birds fly together to help it get free. The squirrel joins the dance. And everyone is happy. The end.'

Priya glanced up at everyone. Did they like her new version of *Swan Lake*? There was a tight knot in Priya's tummy.

But they did like it.

Everybody's eyes were wide and their faces glowed. It was like Priya had been telling a story around a campfire.

'I simply love it,' said Madam Martine. 'You are a magnificent storyteller!'

'You must play Odette the Swan Queen, Priya!' said Lulu. 'You are the animal rescuer! '

Priya felt her cheeks warm, and

the knot in her tummy loosen.

She had never expected to get the lead role. She had imagined the role would go to one of the better dancers, like Bertie or Lulu.

Though, as she had been drawing her story, she had secretly imagined herself as Odette. Odette did feel very ... familiar.

'I agree with Lulu,' said Madam Martine. 'Are you happy with that, Priya?'

Priya nodded, confidence rising inside her.

'Can I be the squirrel?' asked Edmund. 'That role sounds fun!

Chee-chee!' He trotted around with little squirrel paws out in front of him. He pretended to swish his big fluffy tail under his nose and then sneezed. The others laughed.

'Dibs being the magic cygnet!' said Bertie, stretching into a backbend and flicking herself upright. 'That okay with you, Lulu?'

'But Bertie,' said Priya, 'the bird gets to be in the tree! You love climbing trees!'

'Oh yeah!' laughed Bertie. 'Actually, dibs being the bird!'

'Great! I wanted to be the cygnet,' said Lulu. She fluttered about as if she had feathers. 'And I'll wear a cloak of feathers! Madam Martine, can I start sewing it now?'

Madam Martine smiled her big smile.

'I know you are all very excited,' she told them. 'I am too. But Lulu, there is time for dance practice and time for costumes. Right now, we need to do our stretches, and warm-up properly. We don't want any injured animals now, do we? Then who will perform at the Animal Rescue fundraiser?'

CHAPTER SIX

Priya was reading every night with her dad. Rusty. Slow. Tiring.

School was tiring too, because Priya was putting in 200 percent for Mrs Huff. She didn't want to get into any more trouble.

Priya just wished she didn't feel so stupid. And she wished Mrs Huff and the other kids could see all the things Priya was good at.

Priya was good at looking after Mavis, and her other animals. She was good at making up dances. And she was good at dancing. If only Mrs Huff and the others could see her dance!

On Tuesday afternoon, all Priya's dance friends were at dance class. And Priya was with Zac Maxwell, trying her best to concentrate.

Zac's reading lab was a big white room, with a big white desk. Fluoro lights made everything brighter than it already was. Zac himself was big boned and pale skinned, a bit like his lab.

'So, Priya,' said Zac, his big white teeth gleaming, 'how do you feel about reading?'

'It's okay, I guess,' lied Priya. She looked at her feet, and imagined the chassé she should be doing right now around the Stardust dance hall.

'How about we try something simple to begin with?' said Zac.

Priya's mum smiled at her encouragingly.

Priya worked through three worksheets and a set of flashcards. Then Zac cleared his tools away. All that was left was a bare table.

'I'm wondering,' said Zac, 'if there's something that you love, Priya? Something you are passionate about?'

Priya thought it was nice of Zac to try to make friendly conversation, even though she was clearly not reading as well as he expected.

'Animals. Dance. Actually, I am meant to be at my dance class right now,' said Priya.

'Sorry you are missing it,' said Zac. 'I have some homework for you.'

Priya groaned. Then covered her mouth, realising that it was rude to groan.

It's just, she couldn't bear the thought of even more homework.

'What I want you to do before next week, Priya, is find a book about animals. Or dance. A book that makes you feel happy when you hold it. Can you do that for me?' Zac gleamed at her.

A bit of the gleam got under Priya's skin. She nodded. Maybe Zac's reading lab wasn't the worst place in the world.

'The rehearsal went really well, Priya,' Bertie told her on the phone later that evening.

'That's great!' said Priya. Part of her felt as happy as her voice sounded. The other part was miserable because she hadn't been at rehearsal.

'Madam M clapped the entire time,' Bertie went on. 'I swear it looked like her smile was about to snap off. She looked so happy. But we all agreed on one thing, Priya. The dance is much better when you are there.'

'Thanks, Bertie,' said Priya.

When Priya hung up, she and Petit Jeté skipped up to her room.

Priya put on the music medley she had put together for the *Swan Lake* performance. She'd better practise her Swan Queen dance again, to make up for missing class today.

As Priya swept around her room, it truly felt like wing buds were growing on her back. Odette, the animal rescuer, the Swan Queen, will learn to fly!

CHAPTER SEVEN

On Saturday morning, Petit Jeté was lying like a lazy sausage at Priya's feet, bathed in sunshine. Priya wriggled around to sit up in bed.

She was nursing a big book called *Dance Through the Ages*. Her dad had borrowed it for her from the local library. The words were tricky to read.

But Priya found that if she took
a break from the words every now
and then, and gazed at the pictures,
she could actually enjoy the book.

'Priya! Time for your rehearsal in the park!' said her mum, appearing in the doorway. 'Oh, you are reading!' She was radiating with pride.

Priya beamed too. It felt good to make Mum happy.

Dragonfly Park was a giant green field, circled by a rim of old fig trees. Right in the middle of the park was a perfectly round lake, next to a smaller fig tree. A bronze statue of a dragonfly stood alongside the lake.

'Hello, magnificent dancers!' said Madam Martine, her arms open. Priya thought Madam Martine looked like a movie star with her giant sunglasses and big floppy hat.

Priya, Bertie, Edmund and Lulu were there. There were also three kids from the Tiny Tots preschool dance class and two kids from the Starlight class. They would dance the chorus, alongside Priya, Bertie, Edmund and Lulu.

Petit Jeté leaped up, first at Bertie then at everyone else, to give them a hello lick.

'Priya, shall we get started?' asked

Madam Martine. 'Where do you want everyone?'

'I think here is perfect,' said Priya, pointing next to the lake. 'We can use this beautiful little fig tree for the bird.' Priya swept her arm towards a lush patch of lawn. 'The audience can sit here.'

'I better just test out this tree,' said Bertie, swinging herself onto a branch before anyone could stop her. Within seconds, she was three branches up. She smiled down at them. 'It's perfect!' she called.

It didn't matter that Priya had missed rehearsal on Tuesday.

Maybe it was the sunshine
or maybe it was the fresh air.
Whatever it was, the lake rehearsal
went swimmingly!

'I hope lots of people come to see
us dance,' said Priya at the end of
rehearsal, 'to raise lots of money for
the animals.'

'I had an idea ... ' said Lulu.
She whipped away the cloth
from her big basket. Inside were
rolls of paper, paints and sparkly
pens. 'We should advertise! Let's
make posters! We can stick them
everywhere.'

'What a magnificent idea, Lulu,'

said Madam Martine.

The Tiny Tots and the Starlights had to go home. But Priya, Bertie, Lulu, Edmund and Madam Martine sat under the little fig, painting, drawing and colouring.

'How do you spell "lake"?' asked Priya. She was using Lulu's brand new sparkly paint to write with, so wanted to make sure she spelt everything correctly.

'L-A-K-E,' Bertie spelled slowly.

Priya held up her sign when it was finished.

'That's pretty, Priya. What's it meant to say?' asked Edmund.

'*Swan Lake*,' said Priya. A knot of worry tied itself in her chest.

'But that says "Swan Laek". You've switched around the K and the E,' said Edmund.

Petit Jeté licked Priya's cheek, sensing she was upset. Priya had wasted Lulu's special new paint.

Now everyone thinks I'm stupid, Priya thought. Her eyes filled with tears.

CHAPTER EIGHT

Priya stared hard at the ground, wishing her tears would go away. Wishing she would disappear into the earth. But when she looked up, Madam Martine was looking at her warmly. And Lulu was very kind.

'Don't worry, Priya,' said Lulu. 'We can make new letters and can paste them on your sign. No-one will ever know.'

Priya tried to smile. Her smile got bigger as she and the others painted the new letters and covered their fingertips in glitter.

Bertie streaked Priya's face with glitter. And Priya sprinkled glitter in Bertie's hair.

'Priya, shall I walk you to the bathroom to wash all that sparkly stuff off your face?' asked Madam Martine, when Edmund's mum arrived to sit with the others.

Priya was still giggling as she and Petit Jeté walked, and Madam Martine hobbled, under the archway of figs to the bathroom.

'You know, Priya,' said Madam Martine, 'I would have also mixed up the letters in *Swan Lake*.'

Priya thought it was kind of Madam Martine to try to make her feel better. 'But you're an adult. And you're really smart.'

'I am,' said Madam Martine, 'but I am also dyslexic. That means it takes me longer than most people to read. And I am a horrible speller.'

'Dyslexic? Is that a disease?' asked Priya. Her heart thumped harder. Maybe she had the same disease. She didn't know she might have an illness. She just thought she was dumb.

Madam Martine, though, laughed kindly. 'Dyslexia is certainly not a disease. My brain just functions a little differently from other people's. Most people use the left side of their brain for reading and writing. But I mainly use the right side. When I read, I have to decode each sound every time. So it takes me extra energy to understand the meaning. But between you and me, Priya, dyslexia is a bit of a superpower.'

'A superpower?' echoed Priya.

'Because I have always had to try harder than everyone else at reading, it means I try harder at everything. That's partly how I became such a good dancer.'

'I try hard at everything I do too, Madam Martine,' said Priya, nodding. 'Especially reading.'

Madam Martine smiled. 'Also,' she said, 'because I am so used to making mistakes, I am not afraid of mistakes. It means I am not afraid to try new things.'

'Anything else, Madam Martine?' asked Priya.

'Apparently, lots of people with

dyslexia are very creative, Priya,' said Madam Martine. 'I think I might be one of those people.'

Priya found herself hoping she did have dyslexia, just like Madam Martine. Imagine having all those superpowers!

'Madam Martine,' said Priya, 'do you think you can tell my mum about dyslexia when she comes to pick me up?'

Priya's mum's eyebrows shot up when Madam Martine told her about dyslexia.

Mrs Huff's eyebrows also shot up, when Priya's mum told her about dyslexia the next morning.

'Dyslexia?' said Mrs Huff. 'Well, it is a possibility. It might be good to get an assessment.'

'An assessment? Like a test?'

Uh-oh, thought Priya. *I hate tests!*

'Don't worry, Priya,' said Mrs Huff. 'It won't be like a normal test. I think the tests they use can be quite fun. And it's all designed to help you. Mrs Patel, I can put you in touch with an educational psychologist who works near here.'

'Okay then,' said Priya's mum.

'Thank you, Mrs Huff.'

'The psychologist will help me know exactly how I can support you in class,' Mrs Huff told Priya.

Something lifted inside Priya. It felt good knowing there might be a reason why she couldn't read. It felt good knowing that Mrs Huff might be able to help her. And it felt so good to know she might have the same superpowers as the amazing Madam Martine.

The imaginary swan wings on Priya's back unfurled. She felt like she was soaring from the classroom into the afternoon.

CHAPTER NINE

There were lots of good things about the week, and some of those things were these:

1. Imelda, the educational psychologist, had a cancellation the next day and could fit Priya in. Priya was allowed to take the whole day off school to do the tests. Mrs Huff was right. The tests were okay. And Imelda thought that Priya might

well have dyslexia. She'd have to complete her assessment. But for the meantime, she printed out tools to give to Mrs Huff and Priya's parents.

2. Zac Maxwell knew a very kind lady called Audrey Speckles, who knew a lot about dyslexia. Audrey was able to come into Priya's classroom during class time, so Priya wouldn't have to miss dance class anymore.

3. Priya had seen the Stardust posters all around town. Mrs Huff and a few kids from class said they would come along.

Patients at Priya's mum's vet clinic were excited and promised they would come along too. And Priya's mum had managed to get hold of Bob – the man who had found Mavis. He promised he'd be at the dance fundraiser as well.

4. Lulu's *Swan Lake* costumes were magnificent!

5. Madam Martine was able to organise not one but two extra rehearsals during the week. Now the Stardust production of *Swan Lake* was going to be as good as it possibly could be.

On Sunday afternoon, Priya, her
family, Petit Jeté and Mavis made
their way through a sea of people
and animals gathered in the park.

Priya waved to Mrs Huff, who
was there with her chocolate
labradoodle.

Priya's mum spotted Bob in the crowd. The Patels went over with Mavis to say hello.

'Would you mind holding onto Mavis, while we dance, Bob?' Priya asked.

'I'd love to,' said Bob. He hugged Mavis neck.

'I've missed you, Mavis!' he told the alpaca. 'Good news, Priya. My neighbour said she'd be happy to have Mavis in her yard for me. I can take her off your hands!'

Priya's heart squeezed. She loved Mavis as much as she loved all her animals. But she knew this was good news for Mavis.

She gave Mavis a big cuddle around her middle. Bob had rescued Mavis. Mavis should belong to Bob. And Priya already had lots of other animals.

'Can I come visit Mavis sometimes?' asked Priya.

'Of course!' said Bob. 'Anytime!'

The Stardust dancers gathered together under the fig. Madam Martine draped Priya's wings over her t-shirt.

'Magnificent,' whispered Madam Martine looking across at the crowd.

There was a sausage sizzle. A group of violin players performed gypsy music. The crowd danced along.

When the band finished, the Animal Rescue lady with short red hair took the microphone.

'Now, we are very lucky to have our local Stardust School of Dance here to perform their version of *Swan Lake*! Please give them a warm welcome!'

Priya's heart thumped. Her cheeks warmed. Bertie put her arm around Priya's shoulder.

'Priya's version of *Swan Lake* she

means,' whispered Bertie, before crawling up into the branches of the fig tree.

Everyone took their places. Even the animals in the audience seemed to quiet down as the music from *Swan Lake* began.

CHAPTER TEN

Priya, the Swan Queen, was gathering her animal friends together beside the lake for the final dance. Her cheeks were sore from smiling. She held Petit Jeté.

As the music rose to a crescendo, there was a sudden kerfuffle in the crowd. *Maa! Yip! Yip!*

Mavis came hurtling through the people and animals. A tiny black poodle was at her hooves. There were gasps and cries and barks. The crowd parted.

The Stardust dancers scattered as the alpaca galloped towards them. Bob came puffing after her.

'Mavis! No!' called Priya.

But it was too late. Mavis was in the lake, looking desperate.

'Maaa!' she bleated. At the edge of the lake, the poodle wagged its puffy tail and then wandered off, looking pleased with itself.

Priya passed Petit Jeté to Bertie. Forgetting her wings and costume, she splashed into the lake.

'Priya Patel! What are you doing?' Priya heard her mum call.

But Mavis was all Priya could think about. Thankfully, the water was only knee-deep.

'Come, Mavis,' said Priya, calmly. She put her hand out for Mavis to sniff. Mavis's large eyes blinked at Priya. But she let Priya wrap her arm around her neck and lead her back to the bank.

Everybody clapped. Priya's mum and dad and sister Shaan ran to her. They hugged her.

'That was so brave, Priya!' said her dad.

'We're so proud of you,' said her mum.

Shaan gave Priya an extra tight squeeze.

The music was still playing. A bedraggled Priya finished the dance, alongside Bertie, Edmund and Lulu. Mavis stood, dripping, with Bob and Priya's family in the sunshine.

When the show finished, Priya, Bertie, Lulu and Edmund held hands and took a deep bow. They waved Madam Martine and the other Stardust dancers over for yet another round of applause.

The Animal Rescue lady came towards them with a giant smile on her face.

'What a save! And what a dance!' she said to Priya. Then she turned to the crowd. 'You know what? As well as saving an alpaca from the lake, these dancers have helped us raise a whopping $1,000 for our animals in need. Thank you, everyone for your donation! And thank you to our Stardust dancers!'

The lady reached to the stool beside her, and turned back with a laminated rainbow certificate. She handed it to Priya, and pumped

Priya's hand up and down.

Priya gazed at the certificate. 'Thank you for helping our animals,' Priya read aloud, slowly. She smiled back at the lady.

Priya couldn't think of any certificate she'd rather be given.

THE END

More about the
STARDUST dancers

MADAM MARTINE

Madam Martine has always loved dance. When she was younger, she practised hard for many years and eventually became prima ballerina for the New York Ballet. Sadly, an accident meant Madam Martine could no longer dance. But it was then that she discovered she could always dance in her heart. And that she also loved to teach kids to dance. So she created Stardust School of Dance! Madam Martine loves hot cocoa, swirly dance skirts, and helping her young dancers realise their dreams.

BERTIE BLACK

Psst. Don't tell anyone, but Bertie Black is secretly a ninja. She keeps a secret ninja diary, and spends her spare time practising her awesome ninja moves. She's an aerial-flip specialist. But Ninja Bertie has recently discovered she also loves to dance. Bertie lives with her step family on Blossom Lane, just across the road from the Stardust School of Dance. She loves climbing trees, animals, perfecting her ninja moves and her new friends. She is part of Stardust's Bright Sparks class, with Priya, Edmund and Lulu.

LULU LULLABY

Lulu Lullaby lives with her grandma on Blossom Lane. Her grandma was once a famous ballet dancer, and she's taught Lulu everything she knows about ballet. Lulu knows all the fancy French names for ballet steps. As well as dancing, Lulu loves to daydream. She's also a very caring friend and granddaughter. Lulu dreams of being a famous dancer one day, just like her grandma. She is part of Stardust's Bright Sparks class, with Edmund, Priya and Bertie.

EDMUND FONTAINE

Edmund Fontaine's dad would like Edmund to be a chef, just like him. But Edmund is more interested in dance. Edmund spends rainy Sundays watching his favourite movie, *Singin' in the Rain*, and can perform Gene Kelly's dance routine perfectly. The only time you'll catch Edmund out of his tuxedo and top hat, is when he's wearing his dance clothes. Edmund is a good friend, and an excellent tap dancer! He is part of Stardust's Bright Sparks class, with Lulu, Bertie and Priya.

PRIYA PATEL

Priya Patel is an animal whisperer. She helps animals who are in trouble or need a friend. She and her sister Shaan have lots of pets at home, but Priya's closest companion is Petit Jeté, her sausage dog. Priya's mum is a vet. When Priya isn't spending her free time at Stardust School of Dance practising her moves and hanging out with her friends, she's most likely at the vet clinic helping her mum. She is part of Stardust's Bright Sparks class, with Bertie, Edmund and Lulu.